T0402882

OOL CARS

ASTON MARTIN

VALKYRIE

BY KAITLYN DULING

EPIC

BELLWETHER MEDIA ››› MINNEAPOLIS, MN

EPIC BOOKS are no ordinary books. They burst with intense action, high-speed heroics, and shadows of the unknown. Are you ready for an Epic adventure?

This edition first published in 2024 by Bellwether Media, Inc.

No part of this publication may be reproduced in whole or in part without written permission of the publisher. For information regarding permission, write to Bellwether Media, Inc., Attention: Permissions Department, 6012 Blue Circle Drive, Minnetonka, MN 55343.

Library of Congress Cataloging-in-Publication Data

LC record for Aston Martin Valkyrie available at: https://lccn.loc.gov/2023036159

Text copyright © 2024 by Bellwether Media, Inc. EPIC and associated logos are trademarks and/or registered trademarks of Bellwether Media, Inc.

Editor: Rachael Barnes Designer: Jeffrey Kollock

Printed in the United States of America, North Mankato, MN.

TABLE OF CONTENTS

FLYING AROUND THE TRACK

The roar of an engine rips through the air. The Aston Martin Valkyrie flies around the track. It looks like a fighter jet.

The Valkyrie is a **hypercar**.
Its speed, power, and price are extreme!

ALL ABOUT THE VALKYRIE

ASTON MARTIN RACE CAR IN 1921

The Aston Martin company started in England in 1913. It is known for making sports cars and race cars.

The DB5, V8 Vantage, and Vanquish are famous **models**.
VROOM VROOM
Aston Martin's top-performing cars all begin with the letter "V." This includes the Vantage, Vanquish, and Valkyrie!
V8 VANTAGE
WHERE IS IT MADE?
GAYDON, ENGLAND
EUROPE

The Valkyrie was announced in 2016. But buyers had to wait. Production started in 2021.

Only 150 Valkyries were made. Fans love to see the Valkyrie at car shows!

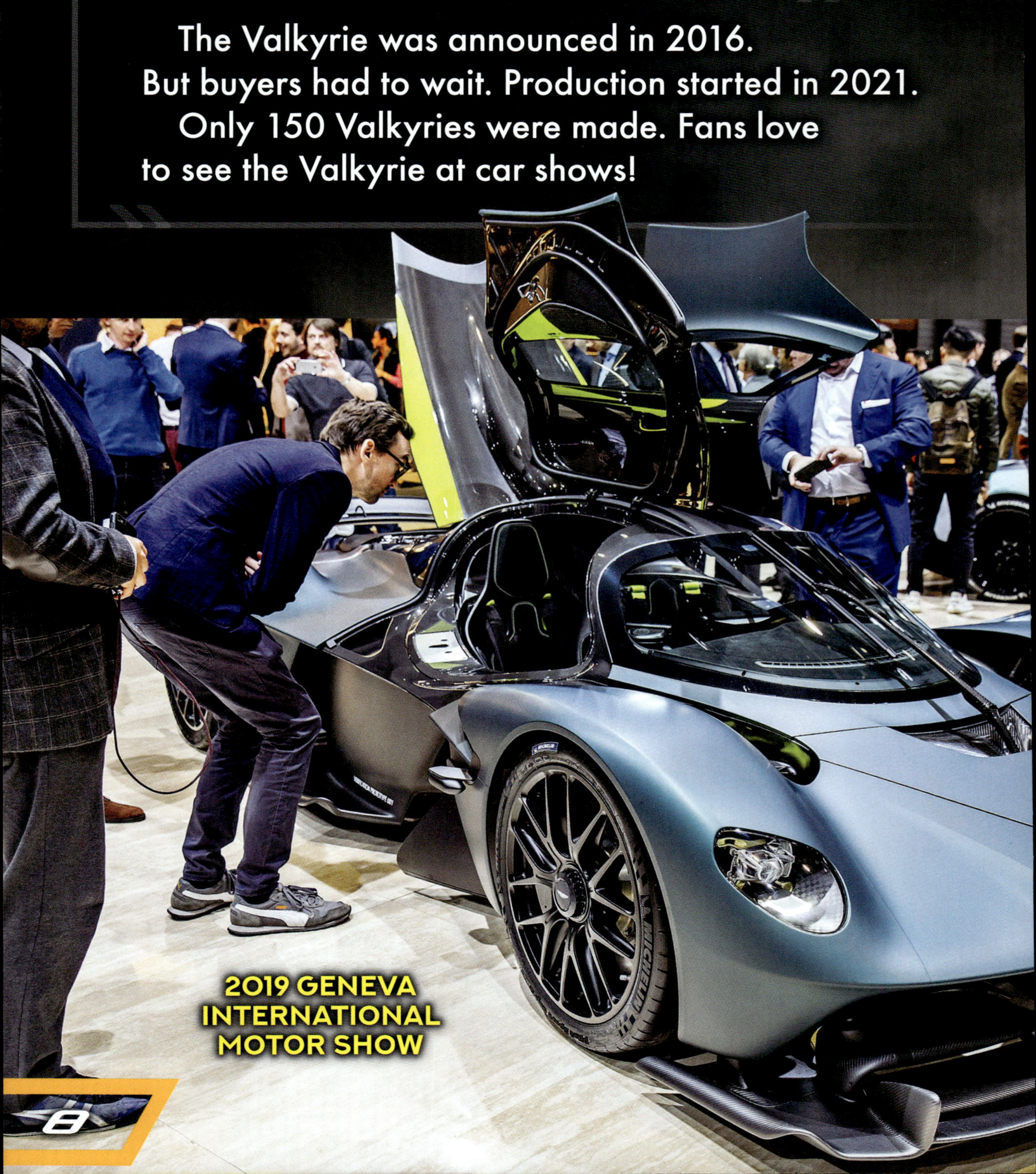

2019 GENEVA INTERNATIONAL MOTOR SHOW

VALKYRIE BASICS

YEAR FIRST MADE	2021
COST	starts at $3 million
HOW MANY MADE	150

FEATURES

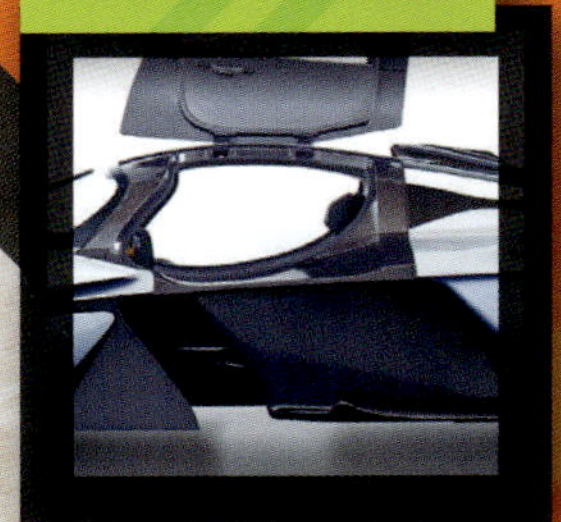

carbon fiber body

roof-hinged doors

Venturi tunnels

PARTS OF THE VALKYRIE

The Valkyrie's heavy engine helps hold the car together. It connects the front wheels to the back wheels.

The Valkyrie is a **hybrid** car. An **electric motor** boosts its power!

ENGINE SPECS

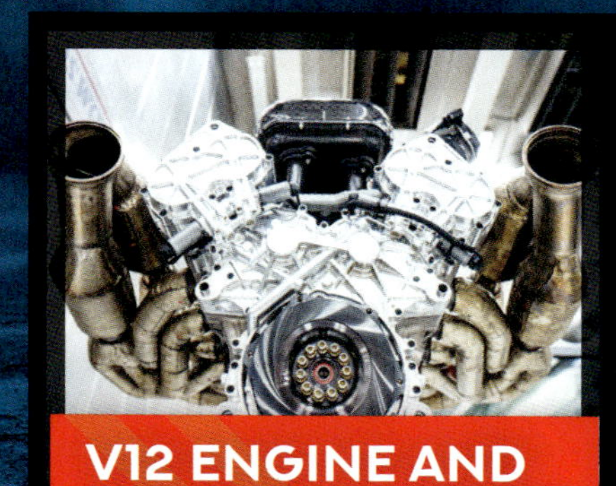

V12 ENGINE AND ELECTRIC MOTOR

TOP SPEED	220 miles (354 kilometers) per hour
0-60 TIME	2.5 seconds
HORSEPOWER	1,139 hp

HIGH-FLYING DOORS

Drivers enter the Valkyrie through doors that open upwards. They look like wings!

The Valkyrie can reach 60 miles (97 kilometers) per hour in 2.5 seconds!

The engine makes a loud growl. It gets so loud, drivers wear noise-canceling headphones!

VALKYRIE
CARBON FIBER

SIZE CHART

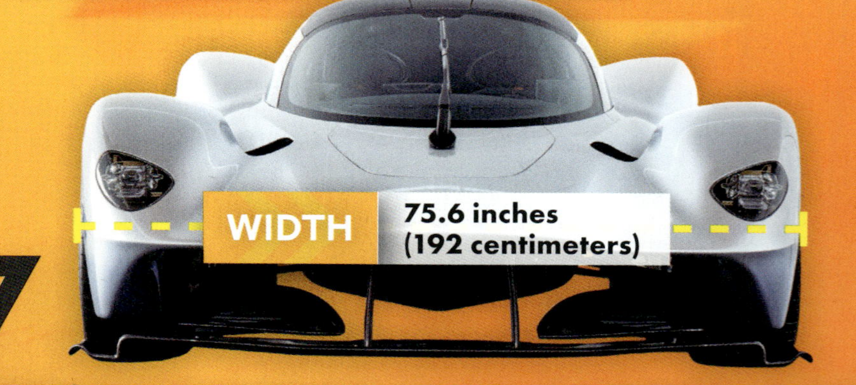
WIDTH
75.6 inches
(192 centimeters)

The body is wide and low. Two Venturi tunnels run underneath. They let air through!

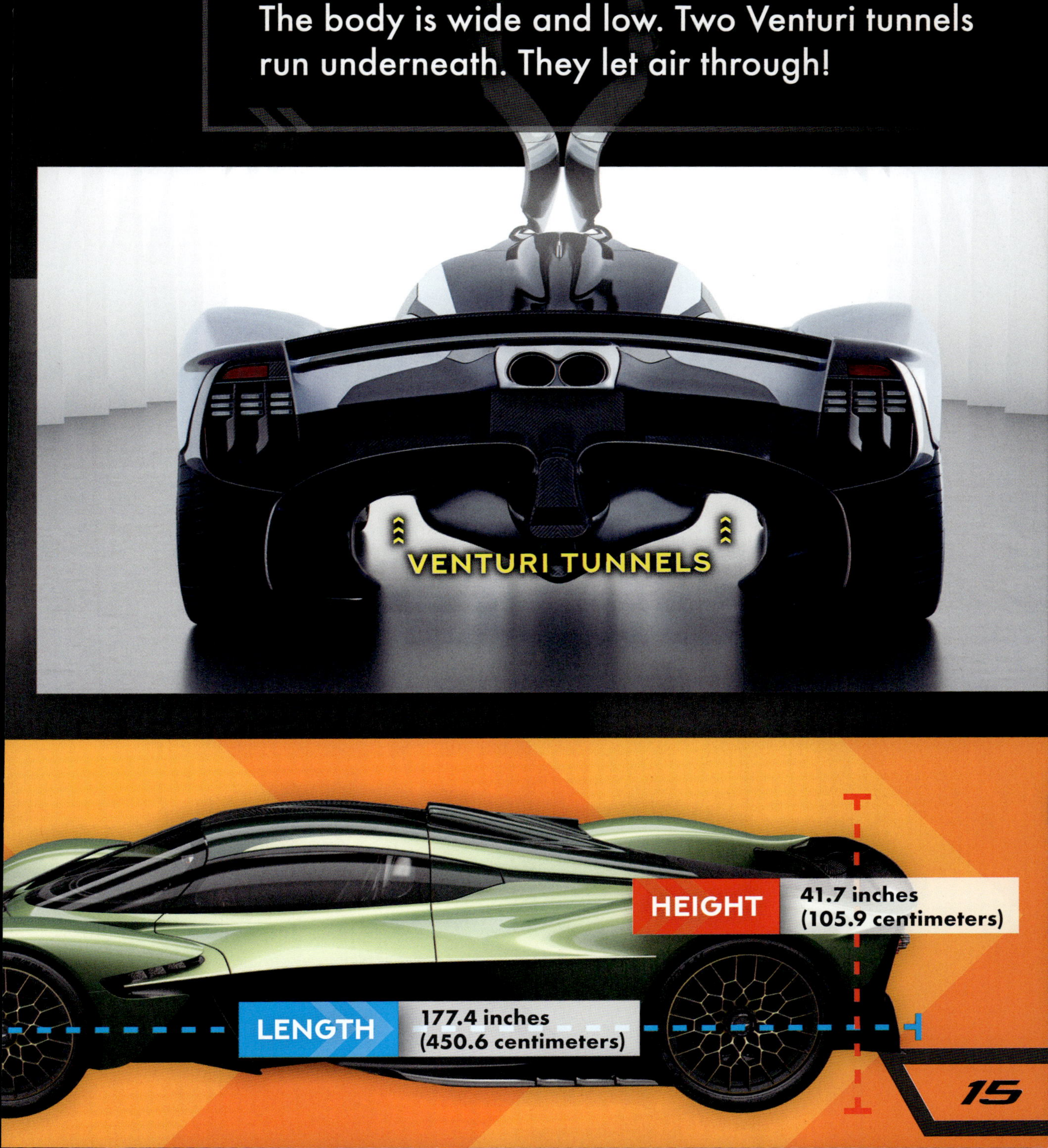

Inside, the Valkyrie looks like a race car. A **racing harness** keeps the driver safe.

SEE AND BE SEEN

The Valkyrie has no mirrors and no back window. Instead, cameras show the driver the road behind them.

The **cockpit** is small. Drivers can remove the steering wheel to get in and out of the car.

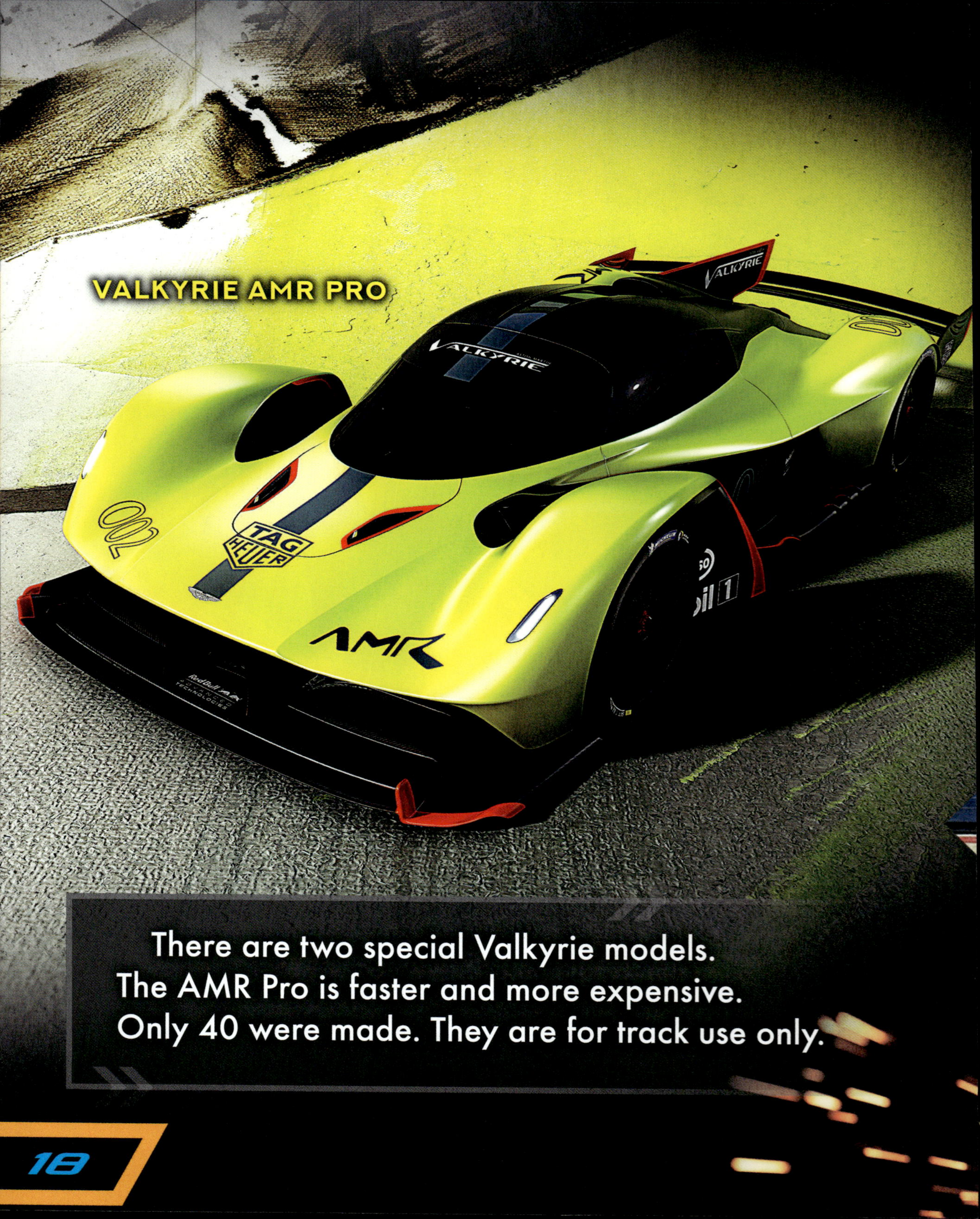

There are two special Valkyrie models. The AMR Pro is faster and more expensive. Only 40 were made. They are for track use only.

The Valkyrie Spider has a removable roof and front-hinged doors.
VALKYRIE SPIDER
‹‹‹ FRONT-HINGED DOORS ›››

THE VALKYRIE'S FUTURE

Every Valkyrie has been sold. But Aston Martin will continue to build hypercars.

In the future, the company will go fully **electric**. They hope to build a flying **vehicle**. For Aston Martin, the sky is the limit!

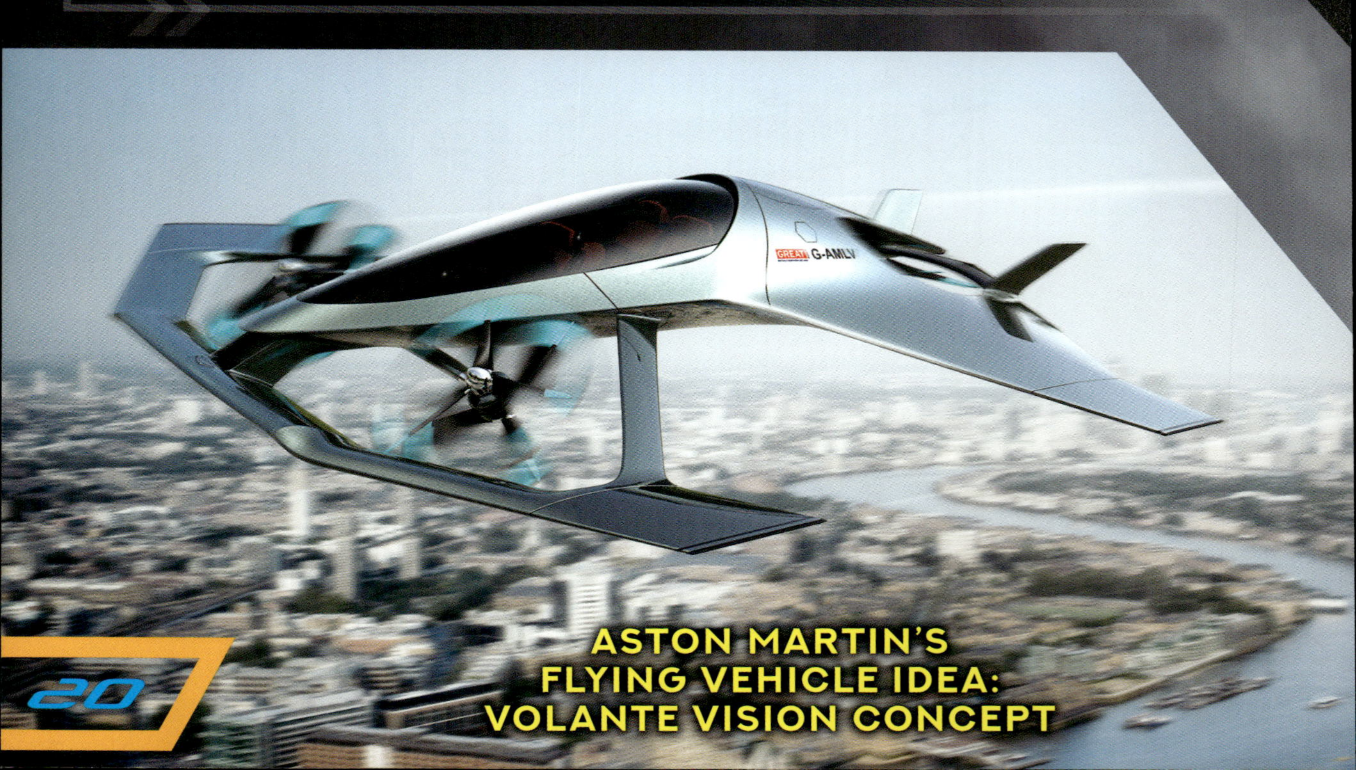

ASTON MARTIN'S FLYING VEHICLE IDEA: VOLANTE VISION CONCEPT

VALKYRIE

GLOSSARY

aerodynamic—able to move through air easily

carbon fiber—a strong, lightweight material used to strengthen things

cockpit—the part of a car where the driver sits

electric—able to run without gasoline

electric motor—a machine that gives something the power to move by using electricity

hybrid—using both a gasoline engine and an electric motor for power

hypercar—an extreme, high-performing sports car that is expensive and made in a limited number

models—specific kinds of cars

racing harness—a kind of seat belt with multiple straps

vehicle—something used to transport people or goods

TO LEARN MORE

AT THE LIBRARY

Robertson, Kay. *Aston Martin Valkyrie*. Minneapolis, Minn.: Kaleidoscope, 2022.

Smith, Ryan. *Aston Martin*. New York, N.Y.: AV2, 2021.

Sommer, Nathan. *Aston Martin Valhalla*. Minneapolis, Minn.: Bellwether Media, 2023.

ON THE WEB

FACTSURFER

Factsurfer.com gives you a safe, fun way to find more information.

1. Go to www.factsurfer.com.
2. Enter "Aston Martin Valkyrie" into the search box and click 🔍.
3. Select your book cover to see a list of related content.

INDEX

aerodynamic, 15
AMR Pro, 18
basics, 9
body, 14, 15
cameras, 17
car shows, 8
carbon fiber, 14
cockpit, 16, 17
company, 6, 7, 20
doors, 11, 19
electric, 20
electric motor, 10
engine, 4, 10, 13
engine specs, 10
England, 6, 7
fans, 8
future, 20
history, 6, 8
hybrid, 10
hypercar, 5, 20
models, 7, 18, 19
name, 7
noise-canceling headphones, 13
number, 8, 18
race cars, 6, 16
racing harness, 16
roof, 19
size, 14–15
speed, 5, 12, 18
Spider, 19
steering wheel, 17
track, 4, 18
Venturi tunnels, 15
wheels, 10

The images in this book are reproduced through the courtesy of: Aston Martin, front cover, pp. 4, 5, 7, 9 (isolated, body, doors, tunnels), 10, 12, 14 (main, carbon fiber, width), 15 (main, length), 16, 17, 18, 19, 20, 21; MrWalkr, p. 3; Motoring Picture Library/ Alamy, p. 6; CTK/ Alamy, p. 8; Independent Photo Agency/ Alamy, p. 11; CJM Photography/ Alamy, p. 13.